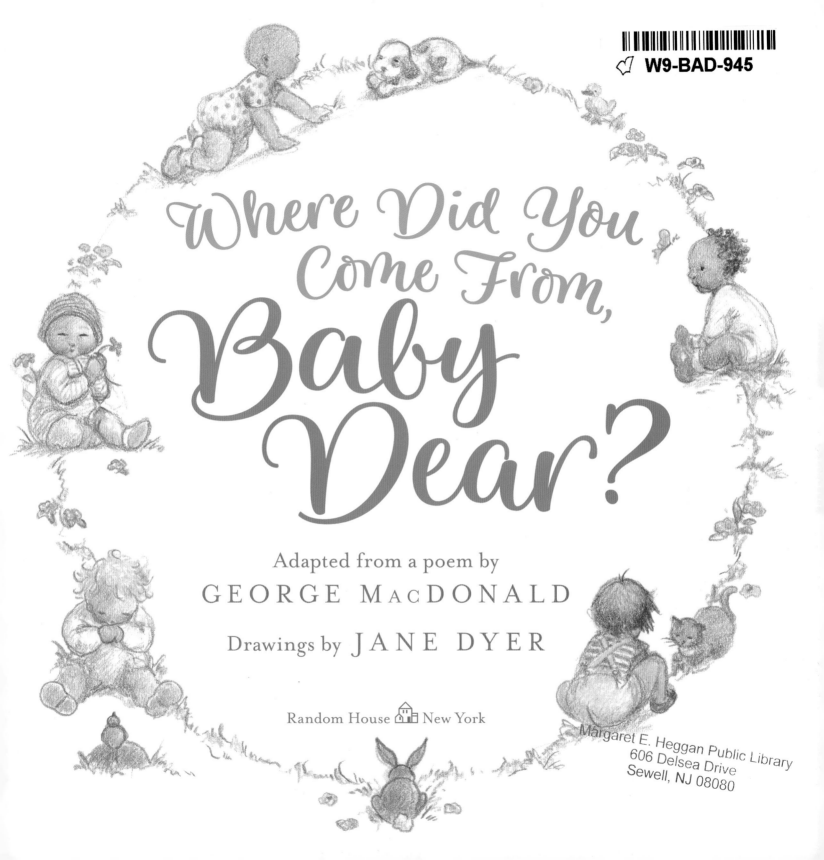

Where Did You Come From, Baby Dear?

Adapted from a poem by

GEORGE MacDONALD

Drawings by JANE DYER

Random House 🏠 New York

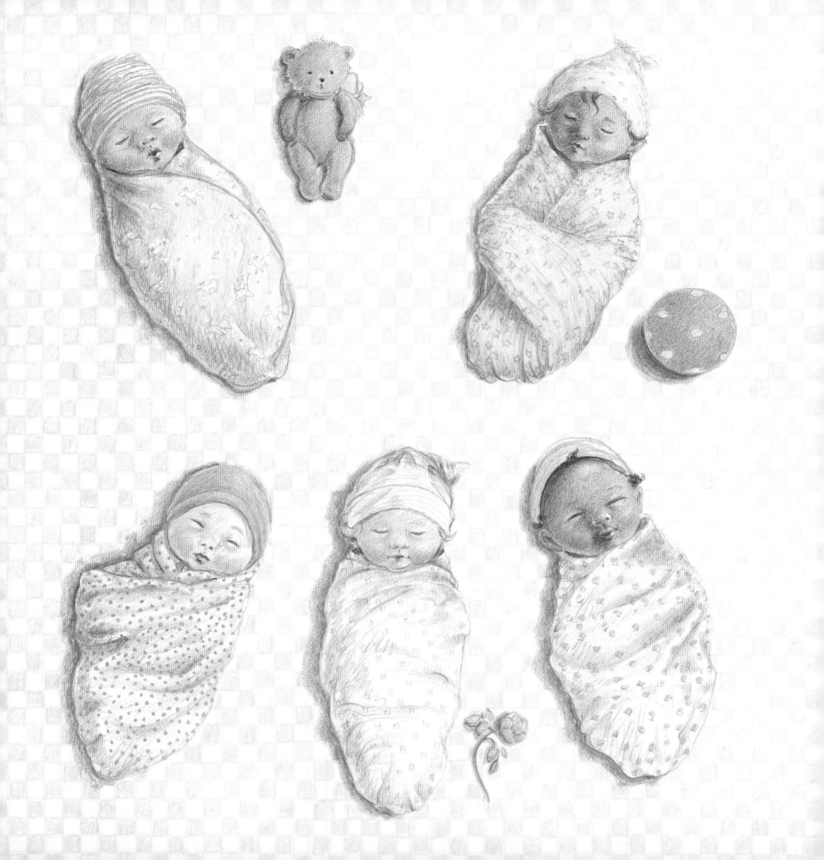

Where did you come from, baby dear?

Out of the everywhere

into the here.

Where did you get those eyes so blue?

Out of the sky as I came through.

What makes the light in them sparkle and spin?

Some of the starry twinkles left in.

Where did you get that little tear?

I found it waiting when I got here.

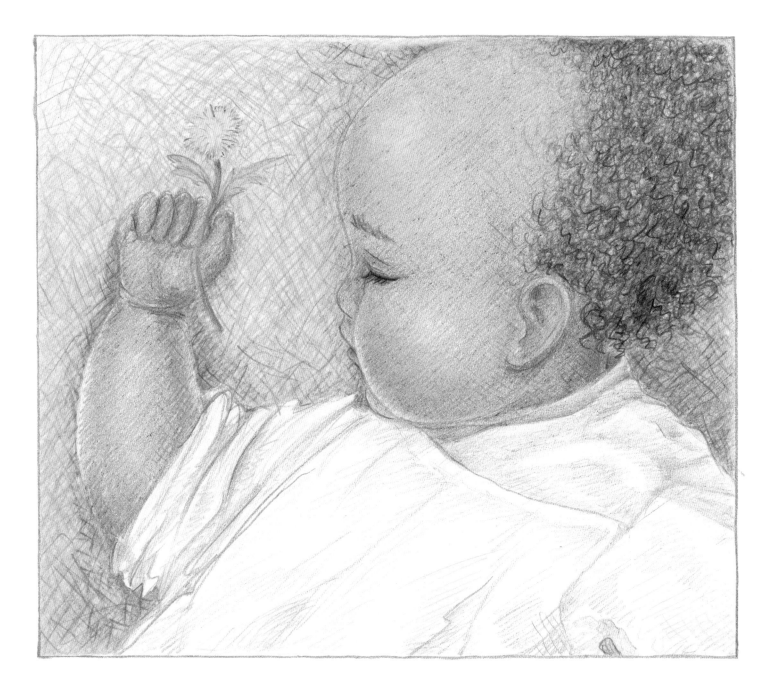

What makes your forehead so smooth and high?

A soft hand stroked it as I went by.

What makes your cheek like a warm wild rose?

I saw something better than anyone knows.

Why that three-cornered smile of bliss?

Three angels gave me at once a kiss.

Where did you get this pearly ear?

God spoke, and it came out to hear.

Where did you get those arms and hands?
Love made itself into bonds and bands.

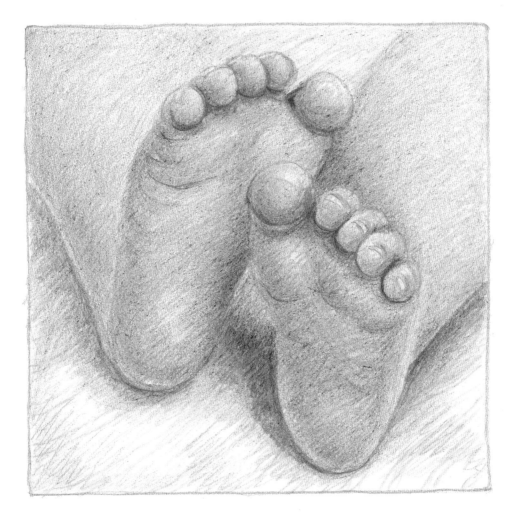

Feet, where are you from, you darling things?

From the same box as the cherubs' wings.

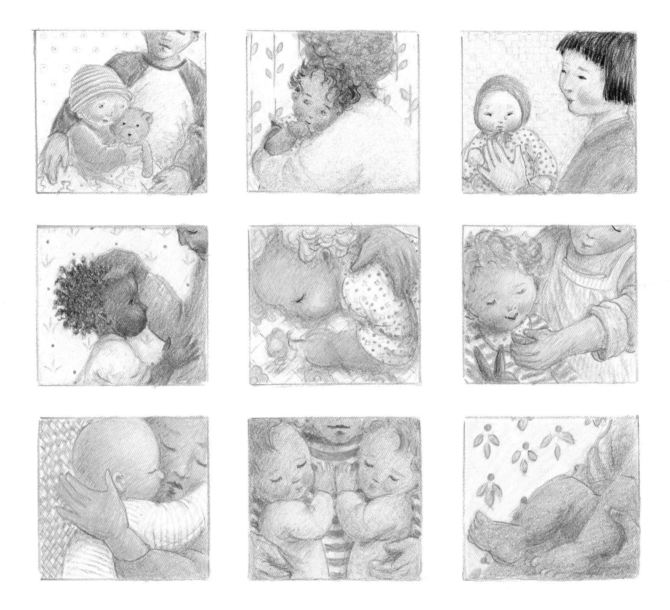

How did they all just come to be you?
God thought about me, and so I grew.

But how did you come to us, you dear?
God thought about you, and so I am here.